Book of Wise Sayings

Selected Largely from Eastern Sources

William A. Clouston

Book of Wise Sayings: Selected Largely from Eastern Sources

The present edition is a reproduction of previous publication of this classic work. Minor typographical errors may have been corrected without note, however, for an authentic reading experience the spelling, punctuation, and capitalization have been retained from the original text.

ISBN: 978-1-64799-165-4

PREFACE

Cynics may ask, how many have profited by the innumerable proverbs and maxims of prudence which have been current in the world time out of mind? They will say that their only use is to repeat them after some unhappy wight has "gone wrong." When, for instance, a man has played "ducks and drakes" with his money, the fact at once calls up the proverb which declares that "wilful waste leads to woful want"; but did not the "waster" know this well-worn saying from his early years downwards? What good, then, did it do him? Again, how many have been benefited by the saying of the ancient Greek poet, that "evil communications corrupt good manners"?—albeit they had it frequently before them in their school "copy-books." Are the maxims of morality useless, then, because they are so much disregarded?

When a man has reached middle-age he generally feels with tenfold force the truth of those "sayings of the wise" which he learned in his early years, and has cause to regret, as well as wonder, that he had not all along followed their wholesome teaching.

For it is to the young, who are about to cross the threshold of active life, that such terse convincing sentences are more especially addressed, and, spite of the proverbial heedlessness of youth, there will be found many who are not deaf to this kind of instruction, if their moral environment be favourable. But, even after the spring-time of youth is past, there are occasions when the mind is peculiarly susceptible to the force of a pithy maxim, which may tend to the reforming of one's way of life. There is commonly more practical wisdom in a striking aphorism than in a round dozen of "goody" books—that is to say, books which are not good in the highest sense, because their themes are overlaid with commonplace and wearisome reflections.

May we not find the "whole duty of man" condensed into a few brief sentences, which have been expressed by thoughtful men in all ages and in countries far apart?— such as: "Love thy neighbour as thyself," "Do unto others as ye would that they should do unto you." The chief themes of all teachers of morality are: benevolence and beneficence; tolerance of the opinions of others; self-control; the acquisition of knowledge—that jewel beyond price; the true uses of wealth; the advantages of resolute, manly exertion; the dignity of labour; the futility of worldly pleasures; the fugacity of time; man's individual insignificance. They are never weary of inculcating taciturnity in preference to loquacity, and the virtues of patience and resignation. They iterate and reiterate the fact that true happiness is to be found only in contentment; and they administer consolation and infuse hope by reminding us that as dark days are followed by bright days, so times of bitter adversity are followed by seasons of sweet prosperity; and thus, like the immortal Sir Hudibras, when "in doleful dumps", we may "cheer ourselves with ends of verse, and sayings of philosophers."

In the following small selection of aphorisms, a considerable proportion are drawn from Eastern literature. Indian wisdom is represented by passages from the great epics, the Mahābhārata and the Rāmāyana; the Panchatantra and the Hitopadesa, two Sanskrit versions of the famous collection of apologues known in Europe as the Fables of Bidpaï, or Pilpay; the Dharma-sastra of Manu; Bhāravi, Māgha, Bhartrihari, and other Hindu poets. Specimens of the mild teachings of Buddha and his more notable followers are taken from the Dhammapada (Path of Virtue) and other canonical works; pregnant sayings of the Jewish Fathers, from the Talmud; Moslem moral philosophy is represented by extracts from Arabic and Persian writers (among the great poets of Persia are, Firdausī, Sa'dī, Hāfiz, Nizāmī, Omar Khayyām, Jāmī); while the proverbial wisdom of the Chinese and the didactic writings of the sages of Burmah are also occasionally cited.

The ordinary reader will probably be somewhat surprised to discover in the aphorisms of the ancient Greeks and

Hindus several close parallels to the doctrines of the Old and New Testaments, and he will have reasoned justly if he conclude that the so-called "heathens" could have derived their spiritual light only from the same Source as that which inspired the Hebrew prophets and the Christian apostles.

Among English writers of aphorisms Francis Bacon, Lord Verulam, is pre-eminent, but none of his pithy sentences find place here, because they are procurable in many inexpensive forms, (e.g., Counsels from my Lord Bacon, 1892), and must be familiar to what is termed "the average general reader." The Enchiridion of Frances Quarles and the Resolves of Owen Feltham are, however, laid under contribution, as also Robert Chamberlain, an author who is probably unknown to many pluming themselves on their thorough acquaintance with English literature, some of whose aphorisms (published in 1638, under the title of Nocturnal Lucubrations) I have deemed worthy of reproduction.

In more modern times, with the sole exception of William Hazlitt, our country has produced no very successful writer of aphorisms. Colton's Lacon; or, Many Things in Few Words, Addressed to Those who Think, went through several editions soon after its first publication in 1820; it is described by Mr. John Morley—and not unfairly—as being "so vapid, so wordy, so futile as to have a place among those books which dispense with parody"; it is "an awful example to anyone who is tempted to try his hand at an aphorism." Mr. Morley is hardly less severe in speaking of the "Thoughts" in Theophrastus Such: "the most insufferable of all deadly-lively prosing in our sublunary world." However this may be, assuredly other works of the author of Adam Bede will be found to furnish many examples of admirable apothegms.

It only remains to add that, bearing in mind that a great collection of gravities commonly proves quite as wearisome reading as a large compilation of gaieties, or facetiæ, I have confined my selection of "sayings of the wise" within the limits of a pocket-volume.

W. A. C.

BOOK OF WISE SAYINGS

1

The enemies which rise within the body, hard to be overcome—thy evil passions—should manfully be fought: he who conquers these is equal to the conquerors of worlds.

Bhāravi

2

If passion gaineth the mastery over reason, the wise will not count thee amongst men.

Firdausi

3

Knowledge is destroyed by associating with the base; with equals equality is gained, and with the distinguished, distinction.

Hitopadesa

4

Dost thou desire that thine own heart should not suffer, redeem thou the sufferer from the bonds of misery.

Sa'dī

5

To friends and eke to foes true kindness show;
No kindly heart unkindly deeds will do;

Harshness will alienate a bosom friend.
And kindness reconcile a deadly foe.

Omar Khayyām

6

There is no greater grief in misery than to turn our thoughts back to happier times.[1]

Dante

7

We in reality only know when we doubt a little. With knowledge comes doubt.

Goethe

8

In the hour of adversity be not without hope, for crystal rain falls from black clouds.

Nizāmī

9

One common origin unites us all, but every sort of wood does not give the perfume of the lignum aloes.

Arabic

10

I asked an experienced elder who had profited by his knowledge of the world, "What course should I pursue to

---

[1] Cf. Goldsmith:
O Memory! thou fond deceiver,
Still importunate and vain;
To former joys recurring ever,
And turning all the past to pain.

obtain prosperity?" He replied, "Contentment—if you are able, practise contentment."

Selman

11

Every moment that a man may be in want of employment, than such I hold him to be far better who is forced to labour for nothing.

Afghan

12

The foolish undertake a trifling act, and soon desist, discouraged; wise men engage in mighty works, and persevere.

Māgha

13

Those who wish well towards their friends disdain to please them with words which are not true.

Bhāravi

14

Reason is captive in the hands of the passions, as a weak man in the hands of an artful woman.

Sa'dī

15

Like an earthen pot, a bad man is easily broken, and cannot readily be restored to his former situation; but a virtuous man, like a vase of gold, is broken with difficulty, and easily repaired.

Hitopadesa

16

The son who delights his father by his good actions; the wife who seeks only her husband's good; the friend who is the same in prosperity and adversity—these three things are the reward of virtue.

Bhartrihari

17

Let us not overstrain our abilities, or we shall do nothing with grace. A clown, whatever he may do, will never pass for a gentleman.

La Fontaine

18

To abstain from speaking is regarded as very difficult. It is not possible to say much that is valuable and striking.[2]

Mahābhārata

19

Pagodas are, like mosques, true houses of prayer;
'Tis prayer that church bells waft upon the air;
Kaaba and temple, rosary and cross,
All are but divers tongues of world-wide prayer.

Omar Khayyām

20

In no wise ask about the faults of others, for he who reporteth the faults of others will report thine also.

Firdausī

21

He that holds fast the golden mean,

---

[2] Cf. James, III, 8

And lives contentedly between
The little and the great,
Feels not the wants that pinch the poor,
Nor plagues that haunt the rich man's door,
Embittering all his state.

Horace

22

Nothing is more becoming a man than silence. It is not the preaching but the practice which ought to be considered as the more important. A profusion of words is sure to lead to error.

Talmud

23

Consider, and you will find that almost all the transactions of the time of Vespasian differed little from those of the present day. You there find marrying and giving in marriage, educating children, sickness, death, war, joyous holidays, traffic, agriculture, flatterers, insolent pride, suspicions, laying of plots, longing for the death of others, newsmongers, lovers, misers, men canvassing for consulship—yet all these passed away, and are nowhere.

M. Aurelius

24

The friendship of the bad is like the shade of some precipitous bank with crumbling sides, which, falling, buries him who is beneath.

Bhāravi

25

His action no applause invites
Who simply good with good repays;

He only justly merits praise
Who wrongful deeds with kind requites.[3]

Panchatantra

26

Death comes, and makes a man his prey,
A man whose powers are yet unspent;
Like one on gathering flowers intent,
Whose thoughts are turned another way.
Begin betimes to practise good,
Lest fate surprise thee unawares
Amid thy round of schemes and cares;
To-morrow's task to-day conclude.[4]

Mahābhārata

27

Let a man's talents or virtues be what they may, we feel satisfaction in his society only as he is satisfied in himself. We cannot enjoy the good qualities of a friend if he seems to be none the better for them.

Hazlitt

28

It was a false maxim of Domitian that he who would gain the people of Rome must promise all things and perform nothing. For when a man is known to be false in his word, instead of a column, which he might be by keeping it, for others to rest upon, he becomes a reed, which no man will vouchsafe to lean upon. Like a floating island, when we come next day to seek it, it is carried from the place we left it in, and, instead of earth to build upon, we find nothing but inconstant and deceiving waves.

Feltham

---

[3] Matt. V, 43, 44
[4] Eccles. IX, 10; XII, 1

29

He is not dead who departs this life with high fame; dead is he, though living, whose brow is branded with infamy.

Tieck

30

In the height of thy prosperity expect adversity, but fear it not. If it come not, thou art the more sweetly possessed of the happiness thou hast, and the more strongly confirmed. If it come, thou art the more gently dispossessed of the happiness thou hadst, and the more firmly prepared.

Quarles

31

A prudent man will not discover his poverty, his self-torments, the disorders of his house, his uneasiness, or his disgrace.

Hitopadesa

32

Men are of three different capacities: one understands intuitively; another understands so far as it is explained; and a third understands neither of himself nor by explanation. The first is excellent, the second, commendable, and the third, altogether useless.

Machiavelli

33

It is difficult to understand men, but still harder to know them thoroughly.

Schiller

34

Worldly fame and pleasure are destructive to the virtue of

the mind; anxious thoughts and apprehensions are injurious to the health of the body.

Chinese

35

Alas, for him who is gone and hath done no good work! The trumpet of march has sounded, and his load was not bound on.

Persian

36

Human experience, like the stern-lights of a ship at sea, illumines only the path which we have passed over.

Coleridge

37

Man is an actor who plays various parts:
First comes a boy, then out a lover starts;
His garb is changed for, lo! a beggar's rags;
Then he's a merchant with full money-bags;
Anon, an aged sire, wrinkled and lean;
At last Death drops the curtain on the scene.[5]

Bhartrihari

38

Through avarice a man loses his understanding, and by his thirst for wealth he gives pain to the inhabitants of both worlds.

Hitopadesa

39

Men soon the faults of others learn,

---

[5] Cf. Shakspeare: "All the world's a stage," etc.—As You Like It, Act II, sc. 7

A few their virtues, too, find out;
But is there one—I have a doubt—
Who can his own defects discern?

Sanskrit

40

In learning, age and youth go for nothing; the best informed take the precedence.

Chinese

41

Mention not a blemish which is thy own in detraction of a neighbour.

Talmud

42

Affairs succeed by patience, and he that is hasty falleth headlong.

Sa'dī

43

A man who has learnt little grows old like an ox: his flesh grows, but his knowledge does not grow.

Dhammapada

44

Unsullied poverty is always happy, while impure wealth brings with it many sorrows.

Chinese

45

Both white and black acknowledge women's sway,

So much the better and the wiser too,
Deeming it most convenient to obey,
Or possibly they might their folly rue.[6]

Persian

46

We are never so much disposed to quarrel with others as when we are dissatisfied with ourselves.

Hazlitt

47

No one is more profoundly sad than he who laughs too much.

Richter

48

The heaven that rolls around cries aloud to you while it displays its eternal beauties, and yet your eyes are fixed upon the earth alone.

Dante

49

This world is a beautiful book, but of little use to him who cannot read it.

Goldoni

50

Sorrows are like thunder-clouds: in the distance they look black, over our heads, hardly gray.

Richter

---

[6] Cf. Pope:
Would men but follow what the sex advise,
All things would prosper, all the world grow wise.

51

The gem cannot be polished without friction, nor man perfected without trials.

Chinese

52

Health is the greatest gift, contentedness the best riches.

Dhammapada

53

Great and unexpected successes are often the cause of foolish rushing into acts of extravagance.

Demosthenes

54

Let none with scorn a suppliant meet,
Or from the door untended spurn
A dog; an outcast kindly treat;
And so thou shalt be blest in turn.

Mahābhārata

55

Choose knowledge, if thou desirest a blessing from the Universal Provider; for the ignorant man cannot raise himself above the earth, and it is by knowledge that thou must render thy soul praiseworthy.

Firdausī

56

Good fortune is a benefit to the wise, but a curse to the foolish.

Chinese

57

In this thing one man is superior to another, that he is better able to bear adversity and prosperity.

Philemon

58

The rays of happiness, like those of light, are colourless when unbroken.

Longfellow

59

There are three things which, in great quantity, are bad, and, in little, very good: leaven, salt, and liberality.

Talmud

60

Who aims at excellence will be above mediocrity; who aims at mediocrity will be far short of it.

Burmese

61

Keep thy heart afar from sorrow, and be not anxious about the trouble which is not yet come.

Firdausī

62

If thy garments be clean and thy heart be foul, thou needest no key to the door of hell.

Sa'dī

63

We ought never to mock the wretched, for who can be sure of being always happy?

La Fontaine

64

To those who err in judgment, not in will, anger is gentle.

Sophocles

65

Not only is the old man twice a child, but also the man who is drunk.

Plato

66

Wrapt up in error is the human mind,
And human bliss is ever insecure;
Know we what fortune yet remains behind?
Know we how long the present shall endure?

Pindar

67

A wise man adapts himself to circumstances, as water shapes itself to the vessel that contains it.

Chinese

68

He who formerly was reckless and afterwards became sober brightens up this world like the moon when freed from clouds.

Dhammapada

69

When a base fellow cannot vie with another in merit he will attack him with malicious slander.

Sa'dī

70

If a man be not so happy as he desires, let this be his comfort—he is not so wretched as he deserves.

R. Chamberlain

71

In conversation humour is more than wit, easiness, more than knowledge; few desire to learn, or to think they need it; all desire to be pleased, or, if not, to be easy.

Sir W. Temple

72

The greatest men sometimes overshoot themselves, but then their very mistakes are so many lessons of instruction.

Tom Browne

73

We may be as good as we please, if we please to be good.

Barrow

74

The round of a passionate man's life is in contracting debts in his passion which his virtue obliges him to pay. He spends his time in outrage and acknowledgment, injury and reparation.

Johnson

75

To reprehend well is the most necessary and the hardest part of friendship. Who is it that does not sometimes merit a check, and yet how few will endure one? Yet wherein can a friend more unfold his love than in preventing dangers before their birth, or in bringing a man to safety who is travelling on the road to ruin? I grant there is a manner of reprehending which turns a benefit into an injury, and then it both strengthens error and wounds the giver. When thou chidest thy wandering friend do it secretly, in season, in love, not in the ear of a popular convention, for oftentimes the presence of a multitude makes a man take up an unjust defence, rather than fall into a just shame.

Feltham

76

I put no account on him who esteems himself just as the popular breath may chance to raise him.

Goethe

77

He who seeks wealth sacrifices his own pleasure, and, like him who carries burdens for others, bears the load of anxiety.

Hitopadesa

78

Circumspection in calamity; mercy in greatness; good speeches in assemblies; fortitude in adversity: these are the self-attained perfections of great souls.

Hitopadesa

79

The best preacher is the heart; the best teacher is time; the best book is the world; the best friend is God.

Talmud

80

A woman will not throw away a garland, though soiled, which her lover gave: not in the object lies a present's worth, but in the love which it was meant to mark.

Bhāravi

81

Men who have not observed discipline, and have not gained treasure in their youth, perish like old herons in a lake without fish.

Dhammapada

82

As drops of bitter medicine, though minute, may have a salutary force, so words, though few and painful, uttered seasonably, may rouse the prostrate energies of those who meet misfortune with despondency.

Bhāravi

83

There are three whose life is no life: he who lives at another's table; he whose wife domineers over him; and he who suffers bodily affliction.

Talmud

84

Let thy words between two foes be such that if they were to become friends thou shouldst not be ashamed.

Sa'dī

85

An indiscreet man is more hurtful than an ill-natured one; for as the latter will only attack his enemies, and those he wishes ill to, the other injures indifferently both his friends and foes.

Addison

86

A man of quick and active wit
For drudgery is more unfit,
Compared to those of duller parts,
Than running nags are to draw carts.

Butler

87

All affectation is the vain and ridiculous attempt of poverty to appear rich.

Lavater

88

There never was, there never will be, a man who is always praised, or a man who is always blamed.

Dhammapada

89

A good man's intellect is piercing, yet inflicts no wound; his actions are deliberate, yet bold; his heart is warm, but never burns; his speech is eloquent, yet ever true.

Māgha

90

He who can feel ashamed will not readily do wrong.

Talmud

91

A stranger who is kind is a kinsman; an unkind kinsman is a stranger.

Hitopadesa

92

The good to others kindness show,
And from them no return exact;
The best and greatest men, they know,
Thus ever nobly love to act.[7]

Mahābhārata

93

Trees loaded with fruit are bent down; the clouds when charged with fresh rain hang down near the earth: even so good men are not uplifted through prosperity. Such is the natural character of the liberal.

Bhartrihari

94

The man who neither gives in charity nor enjoys his wealth, which every day increases, breathes, indeed, like the bellows of a smith, but cannot be said to live.

Hitopadesa

95

That energy which veils itself in mildness is most effective of its object.

Māgha

---

[7] Cf. Luke, VI, 34, 35

96

Our writings are like so many dishes, our readers, our guests, our books, like beauty—that which one admires another rejects; so we are approved as men's fancies are inclined.... As apothecaries, we make new mixtures every day, pour out of one vessel into another; and as those old Romans robbed all cities of the world to set out their bad-cited Rome, we skim off the cream of other men's wits, pick the choice flowers of their tilled gardens, to set out our own sterile plots. We weave the same web still, twist the same rope again and again; or, if it be a new invention, 'tis but some bauble or toy, which idle fellows write, for as idle fellows to read.[8]

Burton

97

It is our follies that make our lives uncomfortable. Our errors of opinion, our cowardly fear of the world's worthless censure, and our eagerness after unnecessary gold have hampered the way of virtue, and made it far more difficult than, in itself, it is.

Feltham

98

There is not half so much danger in the desperate sword of a known foe as in the smooth insinuations of a pretended friend.

R. Chamberlain

---

[8] Ferriar has pointed out, in his Illustrations of Sterne, how these passages from Burton's Anatomy of Melancholy have been boldly plagiarised in the introduction to the fragment on Whiskers in Tristram Shandy: "Shall we for ever make new books as apothecaries make new mixtures, by only pouring out of one vessel into another? Are we for ever to be twisting and untwisting the same rope?" And Dr. Johnson, who was a great admirer of Burton, adopts the illustration of the plundering Romans in his Rambler, No. 143

99

Nothing is so oppressive as a secret; it is difficult for ladies to keep it long, and I know even in this matter a good number of men who are women.

La Fontaine

100

All kinds of beauty do not inspire love: there is a kind of it which pleases only the sight, but does not captivate the affections.

Cervantes

101

Contentment consisteth not in heaping more fuel, but in taking away some fire.

Fuller

102

It is difficult to personate and act a part long, for where truth is not at the bottom Nature will always be endeavouring to return, and will peep out and betray herself one time or other.

Tillotson

103

The truest characters of ignorance
Are vanity, pride, and arrogance;
As blind men use to bear their noses higher
Than those that have their eyes and sight entire.

Butler

104

It is better to be well deserving without praise than to live by the air of undeserved commendation.

R. Chamberlain

105

He travels safe and not unpleasantly who is guarded by poverty and guided by love.

Sir P. Sidney

106

Never put thyself in the way of temptation: even David could not resist it.

Talmud

107

Pride is a vice which pride itself inclines every man to find in others and overlook in himself.

Johnson

108

By six qualities may a fool be known: anger, without cause; speech, without profit; change, without motive; inquiry, without an object; trust in a stranger; and incapacity to discriminate between friend and foe.

Arabic

109

Men are not to be judged by their looks, habits, and appearances, but by the character of their lives and conversations. 'Tis better that a man's own works than another man's words should praise him.

Sir R. L'Estrange

110

To exert his power in doing good is man's most glorious task.

Sophocles

111

Those who are skilled in archery bend their bow only when they are prepared to use it; when they do not require it they allow it to remain unbent, for otherwise it would be unserviceable when the time for using it arrived. So it is with man. If he were to devote himself unceasingly to a dull round of business, without breaking the monotony by cheerful amusements, he would fall imperceptibly into idiotcy, or be struck with paralysis.

Herodotus

112

Blinded by self-conceit and knowing nothing,
Like elephant infatuate with passion,
I thought within myself, I all things knew;
But when by slow degrees I somewhat learnt
By aid of wise preceptors, my conceit,
Like some disease, passed off; and now I live
In the plain sense of what a fool I am.

Bhartrihari

113

Time is the most important thing in human life, for what is pleasure after the departure of time? and the most consolatory, since pain, when pain has passed, is nothing. Time is the wheel-track in which we roll on towards eternity, conducting us to the Incomprehensible. In its progress there is a ripening power, and it ripens us the more, and the more powerfully, when we duly estimate it.

Listen to its voice, do not waste it, but regard it as the highest finite good, in which all finite things are resolved.

Von Humboldt

114

All that we are is made up of our thoughts; it is founded on our thoughts, it is made up of our thoughts. If a man speak or act with a pure thought, happiness will follow him, like a shadow that never leaves him.

Dhammapada

115

Depend not on another, rather lean
Upon thyself; trust to thine own exertions:
Subjection to another's will gives pain;
True happiness consists in self-reliance.

Manu

116

If the friendship of the good be interrupted, their minds admit of no long change; as when the stalks of a lotus are broken the filaments within them are more visibly cemented.

Hitopadesa

117

Anger that has no limit causes terror, and unseasonable kindness does away with respect. Be not so severe as to cause disgust, nor so lenient as to make people presume.

Sa'dī

118

Be patient, if thou wouldst thy ends accomplish; for like patience is there no appliance effective of success, producing certainly abundant fruit of actions, never damped by failure, conquering all impediments.

Bhāravi

119

As rain breaks through an ill-thatched house, passion breaks through an unreflecting mind.

Dhammapada

120

Most men, even the most accomplished, are of limited faculties; every one sets a value on certain qualities in himself and others: these alone he is willing to favour, these alone will he have cultivated.

Goethe

121

Poverty, we may say, surrounds a man with ready-made barriers, which if they do mournfully gall and hamper, do at least prescribe for him, and force on him, a sort of course and goal; a safe and beaten, though a circuitous, course. A great part of his guidance is secure against fatal error, is withdrawn from his control. The rich, again, has his whole life to guide, without goal or barrier, save of his own choosing, and, tempted, is too likely to guide it ill.

Carlyle

122

By Fate full many a heart has been undone,
And many a sprightly rose made woe-begone;
Plume thee not on thy lusty youth and strength:
Full many a bud is blasted ere its bloom.

Omar Khayyām

123

The best thing is to be respected, the next, is to be loved; it is bad to be hated, but still worse to be despised.

Chinese

124

To be envied is a nobler fate than to be pitied.

Pindar

125

He only does not live in vain
Who all the means within his reach
Employs—his wealth, his thought, his speech—
T'advance the weal of other men.

Sanskrit

126

If you injure a harmless person, the evil will fall back upon you, like light dust thrown up against the wind.

Buddhist

127

In the life of every man there are sudden transitions of feeling, which seem almost miraculous. At once, as if some magician had touched the heavens and the earth, the dark clouds melt into the air, the wind falls, and serenity succeeds the storm. The causes which produce these changes may have been long at work within us, but the changes themselves are instantaneous, and apparently without sufficient cause.

Longfellow

128

Man is an intellectual animal, therefore an everlasting contradiction to himself. His senses centre in himself, his ideas reach to the ends of the universe; so that he is torn in pieces between the two without the possibility of its ever being otherwise. A mere physical being or a pure spirit can alone be satisfied with itself.

Hazlitt

129

The pure in heart, who fear to sin,
The good, kindly in word and deed—
These are the beings in the world
Whose nature should be called divine.

Buddhist

130

If thou desirest that the pure in heart should praise thee, lay aside anger; be not a man of many words; and parade not thy virtues in the face of others.

Firdausī

131

A wise man takes a step at a time; he establishes one foot before he takes up the other: an old place should not be forsaken recklessly.

Sanskrit

132

The fish dwell in the depths of the waters, and the eagles in the sides of heaven; the one, though high, may be reached with the arrow, and the other, though deep, with the hook; but the heart of man at a foot's distance cannot be known.[9]

Burmese

---

[9] Cf. Proverbs, XXV, 3

133

The life of man is the incessant walk of nature, wherein every moment is a step towards death. Even our growing to perfection is a progress to decay. Every thought we have is a sand running out of the glass of life.

Feltham

134

I have observed that as long as a man lives and exerts himself he can always find food and raiment, though, it may be, not of the choicest description.

Goethe

135

There are no riches like the sweetness of content, nor poverty comparable to the want of patience.

R. Chamberlain

136

'Tis not for gain, for fame, from fear
That righteous men injustice shun,
And virtuous men hold virtue dear:
An inward voice they seem to hear,
Which tells them duty must be done.

Mahābhārata

137

As far and wide the vernal breeze
Sweet odours waft from blooming trees,
So, too, the grateful savour spreads
To distant lands of virtuous deeds.

Sanskrit

138

In this world, however little happiness may have been our portion, yet have we no desire to die. Whether he can speak of life as cheerful and delicate, or as full of pain, anxiety, and sorrow, never yet have I seen one who wished to die.

Firdausī

139

When morning silvers the dark firmament,

Why shrills the bird of dawning his lament?

It is to show in dawn's bright looking-glass

How of thy careless life a night is spent.

Omar Khayyām

140

Be thou generous, and gentle, and forgiving; as God hath scattered upon thee, scatter thou upon others.

Sa'dī

141

In the body restraint is good; good is restraint in speech; in thought restraint is good: good is restraint in all things.

Dhammapada

142

Men say that everyone is naturally a lover of himself, and that it is right that it should be so. This is a mistake; for in fact the cause of all the blunders committed by man arises from this excessive self-love. For the lover is blinded by the object loved, so that he passes a wrong judgment upon what is just, good, and beautiful, thinking that he ought always to honour what belongs to himself, in preference to truth. For he who intends to be a great man ought to love neither himself nor his own things, but only what is just, whether it happens to be done by himself or by another.

Plato

143

A man eminent in learning has not even a little virtue if he fears to practise it. What precious things can be shown to a blind man when he holds a lamp in his hand?

Hitopadesa

144

The first forty years of our life give the text, the next thirty furnish the commentary upon it, which enables us rightly to understand the true meaning and connection of the text with its moral and its beauties.

Schopenhauer

145

Good actions lead to success, as good medicines to a cure: a healthy man is joyful, and a diligent man attains learning; a just man gains the reward of his virtue.

Hitopadesa

146

Purpose without power is mere weakness and deception; and power without purpose is mere fatuity.

Sa'dī

147

Suffering is the necessary consequence of sin, just as when you eat a sour fruit a stomach complaint ensues.

Burmese

148

Riches disclose in a man's character the bad qualities formerly concealed in his poverty.

Arabic

149

Whate'er the work a man performs,
The most effective aid to its completion—
The most prolific source of true success—
Is energy, without despondency.

Rāmāyāna

150

Humility is a virtue all preach, none practise, and yet everybody is content to hear. The master thinks it good doctrine for his servant, the laity for the clergy, and the clergy for the laity.

Selden

151

Authority intoxicates,
And makes mere sots of magistrates;
The fumes of it invade the brain,
And make men giddy, proud, and vain;
By this the fool commands the wise,
The noble with the base complies,
The sot assumes the rule of wit,
And cowards make the base submit.

Butler

152

No man learns to know his inmost nature by introspection, for he rates himself sometimes too low, and often too high, by his own measurement. Man knows himself only by comparing himself with other men; it is life that touches his genuine worth.

Goethe

153

Increase in goodness as long as thou art here, that, when thou departest, in that thou mayest still be joyful. According to our words and deeds in this life will be the remembrance of us in the world.

Firdausī

154

Parents' affection is best shown by their teaching their children industry and self-denial.

Burmese

155

There are three things to beware of through life: when a man is young, let him beware of his appetites; when he is middle-aged, of his passions; and when old, of covetousness, especially.

Confucius

156

He who has given satisfaction to the best of his time has lived for ages.

Schiller

157

I never yet found pride in a noble nature nor humility in an unworthy mind.

Feltham

158

Worldly fame is but a breath of wind, that blows now this way, now that, and changes name as it changes sides.

Dante

159

True modesty and true pride are much the same thing. Both consist in setting a just value on ourselves—neither more nor less.

Hazlitt

160

Never does a man portray his own character more vividly than in his manner of portraying another.

Richter

161

A foolish husband fears his wife; a prudent wife obeys her husband.

Chinese

162

He who devises evil for another falls at last into his own pit, and the most cunning finds himself caught by what he had prepared for another. But virtue without guile, erect like the lofty palm, rises with greater vigour when it is oppressed.

Metastasio

163

Laughing is peculiar to man, but all men do not laugh for the same reason. There is the attic salt which springs from the charm in the words, from the flash of wit, from the spirited and brilliant sally. There is the low joke which arises from scurrility and idle conceit.

Goldoni

164

The woman who is resolved to be respected can make herself be so even amidst an army of soldiers.

Cervantes

165

Petty ambition would seem to be a mean craving after distinction.

Theophrastus

166

It is an old observation that wise men grow usually wiser as they grow older, and fools more foolish.

Wieland

167

Use law and physic only for necessity. They that use them otherwise abuse themselves into weak bodies and light purses. They are good remedies, bad businesses, and worse recreations.

Quarles

168

In some dispositions there is such an envious kind of pride that they cannot endure that any but themselves should be set forth as excellent; so that when they hear one justly praised they will either openly detract from his virtues; or, if those virtues be, like a clear and shining light, eminent and distinguished, so that he cannot be safely traduced by the tongue, they will then raise a suspicion against him by a mysterious silence, as if there were something remaining to be told which overclouded even his brightest glory.

Feltham

169

Every man thinks with himself, I am well, I am wise, and laughs at others; and 'tis a general fault amongst them all, that which our forefathers approved—diet, apparel, humours, customs, manners—we deride and reject in our time as absurd.

Burton

170

Repeated sin destroys the understanding
And he whose reason is impaired repeats
His sins. The constant practising of virtue
Strengthens the mental faculties, and he
Whose judgment stronger grows acts always right.

Mahābhārata

171

If you wish to know how much preferable wisdom is to gold, then observe: if you change gold you get silver for it, but your gold is gone; but if you exchange one sort of wisdom for another, you obtain fresh knowledge, and at the same time keep what you possessed before.

Talmud

172

The man who listens not to the words of affectionate friends will give joy in the time of distress to his enemies.

Hitopadesa

173

It is a proverbial expression that every man is the maker of his own fortune, and we usually regard it as implying that every man by his folly or wisdom prepares good or evil for himself. But we may view it in another light, namely, that we may so accommodate ourselves to the dispositions of

Providence as to be happy in our lot, whatever may be its privations.

Von Humboldt

174

Be very circumspect in the choice of thy company. In the society of thy equals thou shalt enjoy more pleasure; in the society of thy superiors thou shalt find more profit. To be the best of the company is the way to grow worse; the best means to grow better is to be the worst there.

Quarles

175

Assume in adversity a countenance of prosperity, and in prosperity moderate thy temper.

Livy

176

Mark this! who lives beyond his means
Forfeits respect, loses his sense;
Where'er he goes, through the seven births,
All count him knave: him women hate.

Hindu Poetess

177

Be cautious in your intercourse with the great; they seldom confer obligations on their inferiors but from interested motives. Friendly they appear as long as it serves their turn, but they will render no assistance in time of actual need.

Talmud

178

Man, though he be gray-headed when he comes back, soon

gets a young wife. But a woman's time is short within which she can expect to obtain a husband. If she allows it to slip away, no one cares to marry her. She sits at home, speculating on the probability of her marriage.

Aristophanes

179

Hearts are like tapers, which at beauteous eyes
Kindle a flame of love that never dies;
And beauty is a flame, where hearts, like moths,
Offer themselves a burning sacrifice.

Omar Khayyām

180

When thou utterest not a word thou hast laid thy hand upon it; when thou hast uttered it, it hath laid its hand on thee.

Sa'dī

181

To the tongue which bringeth thee words without reason, the answer that best beseemeth thee is—silence.

Nizāmī

182

The man who talketh much and never acteth will not be held in reputation by anyone.

Firdausī

183

Two sources of success are known: wisdom and effort; make them both thine own, if thou wouldst haply rise.

Māgha

184

The worse the ill that fate on noble souls
Inflicts, the more their firmness; and they arm
Their spirits with adamant to meet the blow.

Hindu Drama

185

Opportunities lose not, for all delay is madness;
'Mid bitter sorrow patience show, for 'tis the key of gladness.

Turkish

186

Man is the only animal with the powers of laughter, a privilege which was not bestowed on him for nothing. Let us then laugh while we may, no matter how broad the laugh may be, and despite of what the poet says about "the loud laugh that speaks the vacant mind." The mind should occasionally be vacant, as the land should sometimes lie fallow, and for precisely the same reason.

Egerton Smith

187

The man of affluence is not in fact more happy than the possessor of a bare competency, unless, in addition to his wealth, the end of his life be fortunate. We often see misery dwelling in the midst of splendour, whilst real happiness is found in humbler stations.

Herodotus

188

Love of money is the disease which renders us most pitiful and grovelling, and love of pleasure is that which renders us most despicable.

Longinus

189

He who labours diligently need never despair. We can accomplish every thing by diligence and labour.

Menander

190

Lost money is bewailed with deeper sighs
Than friends, or kindred, and with louder cries.

Juvenal

191

In one short verse I here express
The sum of tomes of sacred lore:
Beneficence is righteousness,
Oppression's sin's malignant core.

Sanskrit

192

A wound inflicted by arrows heals, a wood cut down by an axe grows, but harsh words are hateful—a wound inflicted by them does not heal. Arrows of different sorts can be extracted from the body, but a word-dart cannot be drawn out, for it is seated in the heart.

Mahābhārata

193

To address a judicious remark to a thoughtless man is a mere threshing of chaff.

Hitopadesa

194

All the blessings of a household come through the wife, therefore should her husband honour her.

Talmud

195

Certain books seem to be written, not that we might learn from them, but in order that we might see how much the author knows.

Goethe

196

All that is old is not therefore necessarily excellent; all that is new is not despicable on that account alone. Let what is really meritorious be pronounced so by the candid judge after due investigation; blockheads alone are influenced by the opinion of others.

Hindu Drama

197

One of the diseases of this age is the multitude of books. It is a thriftless and a thankless occupation, this writing of books: a man were better to sing in a cobbler's shop, for his pay is a penny a patch; but a book-writer, if he get sometimes a few commendations from the judicious, he shall be sure to reap a thousand reproaches from the malicious.

Barnaby Rich

198

We rather confess our moral errors, faults, and crimes than our ignorance.

Goethe

199

The angel grows up in divine knowledge, the brute, in savage ignorance, and the son of man stands hesitating between the two.

Persian

200

She is a wife who is notable in her house; she is a wife who beareth children; she is a wife whose husband is as her life; she is a wife who is obedient to her lord. The wife is half the man; a wife is man's dearest friend; a wife is the source of his religion, his worldly profit, and his love. He who hath a wife maketh offerings in his house. Those who have wives are blest with good fortune. Wives are friends, who, by their kind and gentle speech, soothe you in your retirement. In your distresses they are as mothers, and they are refreshment to those who are travellers in the rugged paths of life.

Mahābhārata

201

He that is ambitious of fame destroys it. He that increaseth not his knowledge diminishes it. He that uses the crown of learning as an instrument of gain will pass away.

Talmud

202

While the slightest inconveniences of the great are magnified into calamities, while tragedy mouths out their sufferings in all the strains of eloquence, the miseries of the poor are entirely disregarded; and yet some of the lower ranks of people undergo more real hardships in one day than those of a more exalted station suffer in their whole lives.

Goldsmith

203

It is impossible for those who are engaged in low and grovelling pursuits to entertain noble and generous sentiments. Their thoughts must always necessarily be somewhat similar to their employments.

Demosthenes

40

204

The interval is immense between corporeal qualifications and sciences: the body in a moment is extinct, but knowledge endureth to the end of time.

Hitopadesa

205

If thou lackest knowledge, what hast thou then acquired? Hast thou acquired knowledge, what else dost thou want?

Talmud

206

Be modest and simple in your deportment, and treat with indifference whatever lies between virtue and vice. Love the human race; obey God.

Marcus Aurelius

207

Bootless grief hurts a man's self, but patience makes a jest of an injury.

R. Chamberlain

208

Poverty without debt is independence.

Arabic

209

Just as the track of birds that cleave the air
Is not discovered, nor yet the path of fish
That skim the water, so the course of those
Who do good actions is not always seen.

Mahābhārata

210

He who has wealth has friends; he who has wealth has relations; he who has wealth is a hero among the people; he who has wealth is even a sage.

Hitopadesa

211

Like a beautiful flower, full of colour but without scent, are the fine but fruitless words of him who does not act accordingly.

Dhammapada

212

When men are doubtful of the true state of things, their wishes lead them to believe in what is most agreeable.

Arrianus

213

Most men the good they have despise,
And blessings which they have not prize:
In winter, wish for summer's glow,
In summer, long for winter's snow.

Sanskrit

214

The best conduct a man can adopt is that which gains him the esteem of others without depriving him of his own.

Talmud

215

Whoso associates with the wicked will be accused of following their ways, though their principles may have made no impression upon him; just as if a person were in the habit of frequenting a tavern, he would not be supposed to go there for prayer, but to drink intoxicating liquor.

Sa'dī

216

The loss of a much-prized treasure is only half felt when we have not regarded its tenure as secure.

Goethe

217

The dull-hued turkey apes the gait
Of lordly peacock, richly plumed;
And thus the poetaster shows
When he would fain his verse recite.

Hindu Poetess

218

Knowledge acquired by a man of low degree places him on a level with a prince, as a small river attains the irremeable ocean; and his fortune is then exalted.

Hitopadesa

219

An evil-minded man is quick to see
His neighbour's faults, though small as mustard seed;
But when he turns his eyes towards his own,
Though large as bilva fruit, he none descries.

Mahābhārata

220

Two persons die remorseful: he who possessed and enjoyed not, and he who knew but did not practise.

Sa'dī

221

With regard to a secret divulged and kept concealed, there is an excellent proverb, that the one is an arrow still in our possession, the other is an arrow sent from the bow.

Jāmī

222

The thing we want eludes our grasp,
Some other thing is given; sometimes
Our wish is gained, and gifts unsought
Are ours; these all are God's own work.

Hindu Poetess

223

If a man conquer in battle a thousand times a thousand men, and if another conquer himself, he is the greater of conquerors.[10]

Dhammapada

224

The man who is in the highest state of prosperity, and who thinks his fortune is most secure, knows not if it will remain unchanged till the evening.

Demosthenes

225

Amongst all possessions knowledge appears pre-eminent. The wise call it supreme riches, because it can never be lost, has no price, and can at no time be destroyed.

Hitopadesa

---

[10] Cf. Prov. XVI, 32

226

The shadows of the mind are like those of the body. In the morning of life they all lie behind us, at noon we trample them under foot, and in the evening they stretch long, broad, and deepening before us.

Longfellow

227

He who is full of faith and modesty, who shrinks from sin, and is full of learning, who is diligent, unremiss, and full of understanding—he, being replete with these seven things, is esteemed a wise man.

Burmese

228

If your foot slip, you may recover your balance, but if your tongue slip, you cannot recall your words.

Telugu

229

A vacant mind is open to all suggestions, as the hollow mountain returns all sounds.

Chinese

230

Women are ever masters when they like,
And cozen with their kindness; they have spells
Superior to the wand of the magicians;
And from their lips the words of wisdom fall,
Like softest music on the listening ear.

Firdausī

231

A man cannot possess anything that is better than a good wife, or anything that is worse than a bad one.

Simonides

232

The wife of bad conduct—constantly pleased with quarrelling—she is known by wise men to be cruel Old Age in the form of a wife.

Panchatantra

233

I have often thought that the cause of men's good or ill fortune depends on whether they make their actions fit with the times. A man having prospered by one mode of acting can never be persuaded that it may be well for him to act differently, whence it is that a man's Fortune varies, because she changes her times and he does not his ways.

Machiavelli

234

By nature all men are alike, but by education very different.

Chinese

235

Whilom, ere youth's conceit had waned, methought
Answers to all life's problems I had wrought;
But now, grown old and wise, too late I see
My life is spent, and all my lore is nought.

Omar Khayyām

236

Weak men gain their object when allied with strong associates: the brook reaches the ocean by the river's aid.

Māgha

237

A swan is out of place among crows, a lion among bulls, a horse among asses, and a wise man among fools.

Burmese

238

Whosoever does not persecute them that persecute him; whosoever takes an offence in silence; he who does good because of love; he who is cheerful under his sufferings— these are the friends of God, and of them the Scripture says, "They shall shine forth like the sun at noontide."

Talmud

239

It is intolerable that a silly fool, with nothing but empty birth to boast of, should in his insolence array himself in the merits of others, and vaunt an honour which does not belong to him.

Boileau

240

Ask not a man who his father was but make trial of his qualities, and then conciliate or reject him accordingly. For it is no disgrace to new wine, if only it be sweet, as to its taste, that it was the juice [or daughter] of sour grapes.

Arabic

241

The sun opens the lotuses, the moon illumines the beds of water-lilies, the cloud pours forth its water unasked: even so the liberal of their own accord are occupied in benefiting others.

Bhartrihari

242

We blame equally him who is too proud to put a proper value on his own merit and him who prizes too highly his spurious worth.

Goethe

243

Men are so simple, and yield so much to necessity, that he who will deceive may always find him that will lend himself to be deceived.

Machiavelli

244

Obstinate silence implies either a mean opinion of ourselves, or a contempt for our company; and it is the more provoking, as others do not know to which of these causes to attribute it—whether humility or pride.

Hazlitt

245

If thou desire not to be poor, desire not to be too rich. He is rich, not that possesses much, but he that covets no more; and he is poor, not that enjoys little, but he that wants too much. The contented mind wants nothing which it hath not; the covetous mind wants, not only what it hath not, but likewise what it hath.

Quarles

246

Those noble men who falsehood dread
In wealth and glory ever grow,
As flames with greater brightness glow
With oil in ceaseless flow when fed.
But like to flames with water drenched,
Which, faintly flickering, die away,
So liars day by day decay,
Till all their lustre soon is quenched.

Sanskrit

247

Watch over thy expenditure, for he who through vain glory spendeth uselessly what he hath on empty follies, will receive neither return nor praise from anyone.

Firdausī

248

If thou art a man, speak not much about thine own manliness, for not every champion driveth the ball to the goal.

Sa'dī

249

The potter forms what he pleases with soft clay, so a man accomplishes his works by his own act.

Hitopadesa

250

No man of high and generous spirit is ever willing to indulge in flattery; the good may feel affection for others, but will not flatter them.

Aristotle

251

An ass will with his long ears fray
The flies that tickle him away;
But man delights to have his ears
Blown maggots in by flatterers.

Butler

252

Books are pleasant, but if by being over-studious we impair our health and spoil our good humour, two of the best things we have, let us give it over. I, for my part, am one of those who think no fruit derived from them can recompense so great a loss.

Montaigne

253

He is happiest, be he king or peasant, who finds peace in his home.

Goethe

254

If with a stranger thou discourse, first learn,
By strictest observation, to discern
If he be wiser than thyself, if so,
Be dumb, and rather choose by him to know;
But if thyself perchance the wiser be,
Then do thou speak, that he may learn by thee.

Randolph

255

Being continually in people's sight, by the satiety which it creates, diminishes the reverence felt for great characters.

Livy

256

There is a great difference between one who can feel ashamed before his own soul and one who is only ashamed before his fellow men.

Talmud

257

By rousing himself, by earnestness, by restraint and control the wise man may make for himself an island which no flood can overwhelm.

Dhammapada

258

The best way to make ourselves agreeable to others is by seeming to think them so. If we appear fully sensible of their good qualities they will not complain of the want of them in us.

Hazlitt

259

To form a judgment intuitively is the privilege of few; authority and example lead the rest of the world. They see with the eyes of others, they hear with the ears of others. Therefore it is very easy to think as all the world now think; but to think as all the world will think thirty years hence is not in the power of every one.

Schopenhauer

260

Poesy is a beauteous damsel, chaste, honourable, discreet, witty, retired, and who keeps herself within the limits of propriety. She is a friend of solitude; fountains entertain her, meadows console her, woods free her from ennui, flowers delight her; in short, she gives pleasure and instruction to all with whom she communicates.

Cervantes

261

How can we learn to know ourselves? By reflection, never, but by our actions. Attempt to do your duty, and you will immediately find what is in you.

Goethe

262

Man is supreme lord and master
Of his own ruin and disaster,
Controls his fate, but nothing less
In ordering his own happiness:
For all his care and providence
Is too feeble a defence
To render it secure and certain
Against the injuries of Fortune;
And oft, in spite of all his wit,
Is lost by one unlucky hit,
And ruined with a circumstance,
And mere punctilio of a chance.

Butler

263

There is nothing in this world which a resolute man, who exerts himself, cannot attain.

Somadeva

264

Ere need be shown, some men will act,
As trees may fruit without a flower;
To some you speak with no result,
As seeds may die, and yield no grain.

Hindu Poetess

265

Seven things characterise the wise man, and seven the blockhead. The wise man speaks not before those who are his superiors, either in age or wisdom. He interrupts not others in the midst of their discourse. He replies not hastily. His questions are relevant to the subject, his answers, to the purpose. In delivering his sentiments he taketh the first in order first, the last, last. What he understands not he says, "I understand not." He acknowledges his error, and is open to conviction. The reverse of all this characterises the blockhead.

Talmud

266

How absolute and omnipotent is the silence of the night! And yet the stillness seems almost audible. From all the measureless depths of air around us comes a half sound, a half whisper, as if we could hear the crumbling and falling away of the earth and all created things in the great miracle of nature—decay and reproduction—ever beginning, never ending—the gradual lapse and running of the sand in the great hour-glass of Time.

Longfellow

267

What avails your wealth, if it makes you arrogant to the poor?

Arabic

268

All confidence is dangerous unless it is complete; there are few circumstances in which it is not better either to hide all or to tell all.

La Bruyère

269

It is well that there is no one without a fault, for he would not have a friend in the world: he would seem to belong to a different species.

Hazlitt

270

The mind alike,
Vigorous or weak, is capable of culture,
But still bears fruit according to its nature.
'Tis not the teacher's skill that rears the scholar:
The sparkling gem gives back the glorious radiance
It drinks from other light, but the dull earth
Absorbs the blaze, and yields no gleam again.

Bhavabhūti

271

One man envies the success in life of another, and hates him in secret; nor is he willing to give him good advice when he is consulted, except it be by some wonderful effort of good feeling, and there are, alas, few such men in the world. A real friend, on the other hand, exults in his friend's happiness, rejoices in all his joys, and is ready to afford him the best advice.

Herodotus

272

This body is a tent which for a space
Does the pure soul with kingly presence grace;
When he departs, comes the tent-pitcher, Death,
Strikes it, and moves to a new halting-place.

Omar Khayyām

273

Speak but little, and that little only when thy own purposes require it. Heaven has given thee two ears but only one tongue, which means: listen to two things, but be not the first to propose one.

Hāfiz

274

The natural hostility of beasts is laid aside when flying from pursuers; so also when danger is impending the enmity of rivals is ended.

Bhāravi

275

He who toils with pain will eat with pleasure.

Chinese

276

A day of fortune is like a harvest-day, we must be busy when the corn is ripe.

Goethe

277

The fame of good men's actions seldom goes beyond their own doors, but their evil deeds are carried a thousand miles' distance.

Chinese

278

A subtle-witted man is like an arrow, which, rending little surface, enters deeply, but they whose minds are dull resemble stones dashing with clumsy force, but never piercing.

Māgha

279

It is good to tame the mind, which is difficult to hold in, and flighty, rushing wheresoever it listeth: a tamed mind brings blessings.

Dhammapada

280

The man who every sacred science knows,
Yet has not strength to keep in check the foes
That rise within him, mars his Fortune's fame,
And brings her by his feebleness to shame.

Bhāravi

281

What a rich man gives and what he consumes, that is his real worth.

Hitopadesa

282

He who does not think too much of himself is much more esteemed than he imagines.

Goethe

283

It is a kind of policy in these days to prefix a fantastical title to a book which is to be sold; for as larks come down to a day-net, many vain readers will tarry and stand gazing, like silly passengers, at an antic picture in a painter's shop that will not look at a judicious piece.

Burton

284

With many readers brilliancy of style passes for affluence

of thought: they mistake buttercups in the grass for immeasurable gold mines under the ground.

Longfellow

285

The doctrine that enters only into the ear is like the repast one takes in a dream.

Chinese

286

Adorn thy mind with knowledge, for knowledge maketh thy worth.

Firdausī

287

Men hail the rising sun with glee,
They love his setting glow to see,
But fail to mark that every day
In fragments bears their life away.
All Nature's face delight to view,
As changing seasons come anew;
None sees how each revolving year
Abridges swiftly man's career.

Ramāyāna

288

The good man shuns evil and follows good; he keeps secret that which ought to be hidden; he makes his virtues manifest to all; he does not forsake one in adversity; he gives in season: such are the marks of a worthy friend.

Bhartrihari

289

No one hath come into the world for a continuance save him who leaveth behind him a good name.[11]

Sa'dī

290

Gross ignorance produces a dogmatic spirit. He who knows nothing thinks he can teach others what he has himself just been learning. He who knows much scarcely believes that what he is saying is unknown to others, and consequently speaks with more hesitation.

La Bruyère

291

When you see a man elated with pride, glorying in his riches and high descent, rising even above fortune, look out for his speedy punishment; for he is only raised the higher that he may fall with a heavier crash.

Menander

292

The ridiculous is produced by any defect that is unattended by pain, or fatal consequences; thus, an ugly and deformed countenance does not fail to cause laughter, if it is not occasioned by pain.

Aristotle

293

Happy the man who early learns the difference between his wishes and his powers.

Goethe

---

[11] Cf. 29

294

There is nothing more pitiable in the world than an irresolute man vacillating between two feelings, who would willingly unite the two, and who does not perceive that nothing can unite them.

Goethe

295

Beauty in a modest woman is like fire at a distance, or like a sharp sword: neither doth the one burn nor the other wound him that comes not too near them.

Cervantes

296

We are more sociable and get on better with people by the heart than the intellect.

La Bruyère

297

A good man may fall, but he falls like a ball [and rebounds]; the ignoble man falls like a lump of clay.

Bhartrihari

298

Do not anxiously expect what is not yet come; do not vainly regret what is already past.

Chinese

299

The way to subject all things to thyself is to subject thyself to reason; thou shalt govern many if reason govern thee. Wouldst thou be a monarch of a little world, command thyself.

Quarles

300

If our inward griefs were written on our brows, how many who are envied now would be pitied. It would seem that they had their deadliest foe in their own breast, and their whole happiness would be reduced to mere seeming.

Metastasio

301

There are many who talk on from ignorance rather than from knowledge, and who find the former an inexhaustible fund of conversation.

Hazlitt

302

Whoever brings cheerfulness to his work, and is ever active, dashes through the world's labours.

Tieck

303

Grossness is not difficult to define: it is obtrusive and objectionable pleasantry.

Theophrastus

304

Do not consider any vice as trivial, and therefore practise it; do not consider any virtue as unimportant, and therefore neglect it.

Chinese

305

To bad as well as good, to all,
A generous man compassion shows;

On earth no mortal lives, he knows,
Who does not oft through weakness fall.

Rāmāyana

306

The good extend their loving care
To men, however mean or vile;
E'en base Chándálas'[12] dwellings share
Th' impartial sunbeam's silver smile.

Hitopadesa

307

Let a man accept with confidence valuable knowledge even from a person of low degree, good instruction regarding duty even from a humble man, and a jewel of a wife even from an ignoble family.

Manu

308

We cannot too soon convince ourselves how easily we may be dispensed with in the world. What important personages we imagine ourselves to be! We think that we alone are the life of the circle in which we move; in our absence, we fancy that life, existence, breath will come to a general pause, and, alas, the gap which we leave is scarcely perceptible, so quickly is it filled again; nay, it is often the place, if not of something better, at least for something more agreeable.

Goethe

309

The friendships formed between good and evil men differ. The friendship of the good, at first faint like the morning

---

[12] Chándálas, or Pariahs, are the lowest, or of no caste.

light, continually increases; the friendship of the evil at the very beginning is like the light of midday, and dies away like the light of evening.[13]

Bhartrihari

310

A hundred long leagues is no distance for him who would quench the thirst of covetousness; but a contented mind has no solicitude for grasping wealth.

Hitopadesa

311

The noble-minded dedicate themselves to the promotion of the happiness of others—even of those who injure them. True happiness consists in making happy.

Bhāravi

312

A benefit given to the good is like characters engraven on a stone; a benefit given to the evil is like a line drawn on water.

Buddhist

313

The undertaking of a careless man succeeds not, though he use the right expedients: a clever hunter, though well placed in ambush, kills not his quarry if he falls asleep.

Bhāravi

314

All love, at first, like generous wine,
Ferments and frets until 'tis fine;

---

[13] In many parts of the East there is practically no twilight.

But when 'tis settled on the lee,
And from th' impurer matter free,
Becomes the richer still the older,
And proves the pleasanter the colder.

Butler

315

Safe in thy breast close lock up thy intents,
For he that knows thy purpose best prevents.

Randolph

316

Frugality should ever be practised, but not excessive parsimony.

Hitopadesa

317

He who receives a favour must retain a recollection of it for all time to come; but he who confers should at once forget it, if he is not to show a sordid and ungenerous spirit. To remind a man of a kindness conferred on him, and to talk of it, is little different from a reproach.

Demosthenes

318

Pride not thyself on thy religious works,
Give to the poor, but talk not of thy gifts:
By pride religious merit melts away,
The merit of thy alms, by ostentation.

Manu

319

The empty beds of rivers fill again;
Trees leafless now renew their vernal bloom;

Returning moons their lustrous phase resume;
But man a second youth expects in vain.[14]

Somadeva

320

Shall He to thee His aid refuse
Who clothes the swan in dazzling white,
Who robes in green the parrot bright,
The peacocks decks in rainbow hues?[15]

Hitopadesa

321

A bad man is as much pleased as a good man is distressed
to speak ill of others.

Mahābhārata

322

Every bird has its decoy, and every man is led and misled
in his own peculiar way.

Goethe

323

There is such a grateful tickling in the mind of man in
being commended that even when we know the praises
which are bestowed on us are not our due, we are not angry
with the author's insincerity.

Feltham

---

[14] Cf. Job, XIV, 7
[15] Cf. Matt. VI, 25, 26

324

Too much to lament a misery is the next way to draw on a remediless mischief.

R. Chamberlain

325

There is no remembrance which time doth not obliterate, nor pain which death doth not put an end to.

Cervantes

326

Look not mournfully into the Past. It comes not back again. Wisely improve the Present. It is thine. Go forth to meet the shadowy Future, without fear, and with a manly heart.

Longfellow

327

Plans that are wise and prudent in themselves are rendered vain when the execution of them is carried on negligently and with imprudence.

Guicciardini

328

Every man stamps his value on himself. The price we challenge for ourselves is given us. Man is made great or little by his own will.

Schiller

329

Hath any wronged thee, be bravely revenged. Slight it, and the work's begun; forgive it, and 'tis finished. He is below himself that is not above an injury.

Quarles

330

As gold is tried by the furnace, and the baser metal shown, so the hollow-hearted friend is known by adversity.

Metastasio

331

The rose does not bloom without thorns. True, but would that the thorns did not outlive the rose.

Richter

332

Truth from the mouth of an honest man and severity from a good-natured man have a double effect.

Hazlitt

333

Most virgins marry, just as nuns
The same thing the same way renounce;
Before they've wit to understand
The bold attempt, they take in hand;
Or, having stayed and lost their tides,
Are out of season grown for brides.

Butler

334

The fountain of content must spring up in the mind, and he who has so little knowledge of human nature as to seek happiness by changing anything but his own disposition will waste his life in fruitless efforts, and multiply the griefs which he purposes to remove.

Johnson

335

In all things, to serve from the lowest station upwards is

necessary. To restrict yourself to a trade is best. For the narrow mind, whatever he attempts is still a trade; for the higher, an art; and the highest in doing one thing does all, or, to speak less paradoxically, in the one thing which he does rightly he sees the likeness of all that is done rightly.

Goethe

336

Misanthropy ariseth from a man trusting another without having sufficient knowledge of his character, and, thinking him to be truthful, sincere, and honourable, finds a little afterwards that he is wicked, faithless, and then he meets with another of the same character. When a man experiences this often, and more particularly from those whom he considered his most dear and best friends, at last, having frequently made a slip, he hates the whole world, and thinks that there is nothing sound at all in any of them.

Plato

337

Pleasure, most often delusive, may be born of delusion. Pleasure, herself a sorceress, may pitch her tents on enchanted ground. But happiness (or, to use a more accurate and comprehensive term, solid well-being) can be built on virtue alone, and must of necessity have truth for its foundation.

Coleridge

338

Entangled in a hundred worldly snares,
Self-seeking men, by ignorance deluded,
Strive by unrighteous means to pile up riches.
Then, in their self-complacency, they say,
"This acquisition I have made to-day,
That will I gain to-morrow, so much pelf
Is hoarded up already, so much more
Remains that I have yet to treasure up.
This enemy I have destroyed, him also,

And others in their turn, I will despatch.
I am a lord; I will enjoy myself;
I'm wealthy, noble, strong, successful, happy;
I'm absolutely perfect; no one else
In all the world can be compared to me.
Now will I offer up a sacrifice,
Give gifts with lavish hand, and be triumphant."
Such men, befooled by endless vain conceits,
Caught in the meshes of the world's illusion,
Immersed in sensuality, descend
Down to the foulest hell of unclean spirits.[16]

Mahābhārata

339

There needs no other charm, nor conjuror,
To raise infernal spirits up, but Fear,
That makes men pull their horns in, like a snail,
That's both a prisoner to itself and jail;
Draws more fantastic shapes than in the grains
Of knotted wood, in some men's crazy brains,
When all the cocks they think they are, and bulls,
Are only in the insides of their skulls.

Butler

340

He that rectifies a crooked stick bends it the contrary way, so must he that would reform a vice learn to affect its mere contrary, and in time he shall see the springing blossoms of a happy restoration.

R. Chamberlain

341

The more weakness the more falsehood; strength goes straight: every cannon ball that has in it hollows and holes goes crooked.

Richter

---

[16] Cf. Luke, XII, 17-20; see also 291

342

Learning dissipates many doubts, and causes things otherwise invisible to be seen, and is the eye of everyone who is not absolutely blind.

Hitopadesa

343

Very distasteful is excessive fame
To the sour palate of the envious mind,
Who hears with grief his neighbours good by name,
And hates the fortune that he ne'er shall find.

Pindar

344

A more glorious victory cannot be gained over another man than this, that when the injury began on his part the kindness should begin on ours.

Tillotson

345

Time, which gnaws and diminishes all things else, augments and increases benefits, because a noble action of liberality done to a man of reason doth grow continually by his generously thinking of it and remembering it.

Rabelais

346

Were all thy fond endeavours vain
To chase away the sufferer's smart,
Still hover near, lest absence pain
His lonely heart.
For friendship's tones have kindlier power
Than odorous fruit, or nectared bowl,

To soothe, in sorrow's languid hour,
The sinking soul.

Sa'dī

347

The faults of others are easily perceived, but those of oneself are difficult to perceive; a man winnows his neighbour's faults like chaff, but his own fault he hides as a cheat hides the false dice from the gamester.

Dhammapada

348

Education and morals will be found almost the whole that goes to make a good man.

Aristotle

349

Toil and pleasure, in their natures opposite, are yet linked together in a kind of necessary connection.

Livy

350

Enjoy thou the prosperity of others,
Although thyself unprosperous; noble men
Take pleasure in their neighbours' happiness.

Mahābhārata

351

Neither live with a bad man nor be at enmity with him; even as if you take hold of glowing charcoal it will burn you, if you take hold of cold charcoal it will soil you.

Buddhist

352

In the sandal-tree are serpents, in the water lotus flowers, but crocodiles also; even virtues are marred by the vicious—in all enjoyments there is something which impairs our happiness.

Hitopadesa

353

There is no pleasure of life sprouting like a tree from one root but there is some pain joined to it; and again nature brings good out of evil.

Menander

354

The manner of giving shows the character of the giver more than the gift itself. There is a princely manner of giving and accepting.

Lavater

355

Perfect ignorance is quiet, perfect knowledge is quiet; not so the transition from the former to the latter.

Carlyle

356

Superstition is the religion of feeble minds; and they must be tolerated in an admixture of it in some trifling or enthusiastic shape or other; else you will deprive weak minds of a resource found necessary to the strongest.

Burke

357

Fair words without good deeds to a man in misery are like a saddle of gold clapped upon a galled horse.

Chamberlain

358

There is a rabble among the gentry as well as the commonalty; a sort of plebeian heads whose fancy moves with the same wheel as these men—in the same level with mechanics, though their fortunes do sometimes gild their infirmities and their purses compound for their follies.

Sir Thomas Browne

359

It is a common remark that men talk most who think least; just as frogs cease their quacking when a light is brought to the water-side.

Richter

360

Our time is like our money; when we change a guinea the shillings escape as things of small account; when we break a day by idleness in the morning, the rest of the hours lose their importance in our eyes.

Sir Walter Scott

361

Vociferation and calmness of character seldom meet in the same person.

Lavater

362

Wit and wisdom differ. Wit is upon the sudden turn, wisdom is in bringing about ends.

Selden

363

Real and solid happiness springs from moderation.

Goethe

364

In all the world there is no vice
Less prone t'excess than avarice;
It neither cares for food nor clothing:
Nature's content with little, that with nothing.

Butler

365

Beside the streamlet seated, mark how life glides on:
That sign, how swift each moment goes, to me's enough.
Behold this world's delights, and view its various pains:
If not to you, the joy it shows to me's enough.

Hāfiz

366

The lake no longer water holds—
Off fly the fowls, the lilies stay:
If friends are friends when wealth is gone,
The lily's constancy they share.

Hindu Poetess

367

Let us be well persuaded that everyone of us possesses

happiness in proportion to his virtue and wisdom, and according as he acts in obedience to their suggestion.

Aristotle

368

All property which comes to hand by means of violence, or infamy, or baseness, however large it may be, is tainted and unblest. On the other hand, whatever is obtained by honest profit, small though it be, brings a blessing with it.[17]

Akhlak-i-Jalālī

369

We should know mankind better if we were not so anxious to resemble one another.

Goethe

370

Root out the love of self, as you might the autumn lotus with your hand.

Buddhist

371

Whoever has the seed of virtue and honour implanted in his breast will drop a sympathising tear on the woes of his neighbour.

Nakhshabī

372

Do naught to others which, if done to thee, would cause thee pain: this is the sum of duty.[18]

Mahābhārata

---

[17] See 44
[18] Cf. Matt. VII, 12

A bad man, though raised to honour, always returns to his natural course, as a dog's tail, though warmed by the fire and rubbed with oil, retains its form.[19]

Hitopadesa

374

The man who cannot blush, and who has no feelings of fear, has reached the acme of impudence.

Menander

375

It is the usual consolation of the envious, if they cannot maintain their superiority, to represent those by whom they are surpassed as inferior to some one else.

Plutarch

376

Such as the chain of causes we call Fate, such is the chain of wishes: one links on to another; the whole man is bound in the chain of wishing for ever.

Seneca

377

I do remember stopping by the way,
To watch a potter thumping his wet clay;
And with its all-obliterated tongue
It murmured, "Gently, brother, gently, pray!"

Omar Khayyām

---

[19] Cf. Arab proverb: "A dog's tail never can be made straight."

378

If you only knew the evils which others suffer, you would willingly submit to those which you now bear.

Philemon

379

Children form a bond of union than which the human heart finds none more enduring.

Livy

380

The sweetest pleasures soonest cloy,
And its best flavour temperance gives to joy.

Juvenal

381

To our own sorrows serious heed we give,
But for another's we soon cease to grieve.

Pindar

382

Can anything be more absurd than that the nearer we are to our journey's end, we should lay in the more provision for it?

Cicero

383

Set about whatever you intend to do; the beginning is half the battle.

Ausonius

384

All smatterers are more brisk and pert
Than those who understand an art;
As little sparkles shine more bright
Than glowing coals that gave them light.

Butler

385

No prince, how great soever, begets his predecessors, and the noblest rivers are not navigable to the fountain.

A. Marvell

386

The guilty man may escape, but he cannot be sure of doing so.

Epicurus

387

In everything you will find annoyances, but you ought to consider whether the advantages do not predominate.

Menander

388

Dreams in general take their rise from those incidents which have most occupied the thoughts during the day.

Herodotus

389

Sleeping, we image what awake we wish;
Dogs dream of bones, and fishermen of fish.[20]

Theocritus

---

[20] Cf. Arab proverb: "The dream of the cat is always about mice."

390

A man who does not endeavour to seem more than he is will generally be thought nothing of. We habitually make such large deductions for pretence and imposture that no real merit will stand against them. It is necessary to set off our good qualities with a certain air of plausibility and self-importance, as some attention to fashion is necessary.

Hazlitt

391

There is nothing more beautiful than cheerfulness in an old face, and among country people it is always a sign of a well-regulated life.

Richter

392

From things which have been obtained after having been long desired men almost never derive the pleasure and delight which they had anticipated.

Guicciardini

393

Seest thou good days? Prepare for evil times. No summer but hath its winter. He never reaped comfort in adversity that sowed not in prosperity.

Quarles

394

Every man knows his own but not others' defects and miseries; and 'tis the nature of all men still to reflect upon themselves their own misfortunes, not to examine or consider other men's, not to confer themselves with others; to recount their own miseries but not their good gifts, fortunes, benefits which they have, to ruminate on their adversity, but not once to think on their prosperity, not what they have but what they want.

Burton

395

Some people, you would think, are made up of nothing but title and genealogy; the stamp of dignity defaces in them the very character of humanity, and transports them to such a degree of haughtiness that they reckon it below them to exercise good nature or good manners.

L'Estrange

396

He alone is poor who does not possess knowledge.

Talmud

397

It is not enough to know; we must apply what we know. It is not enough to will; we must also act.

Goethe

398

Words of blame from those who are hostile to a great man cannot injure him. The moon is not hurt when barked at by a dog.

Arabic

399

The value of three things is justly appreciated by all classes of men: youth, by the old; health, by the diseased; and wealth, by the needy.

Omar Khayyām

400

As one might nurse a tiny flame,
The able and far-seeing man,
E'en with the smallest capital,
Can raise himself to wealth.

Buddhist

401

By a husband wealth is accumulated; by a wife is its preservation.

Burmese

402

It is very hard for the mind to disengage itself from a subject on which it has been long employed. The thoughts will be rising of themselves from time to time, though we have given them no encouragement, as the tossings and fluctuations of the sea continue several hours after the winds are laid.

Addison

403

Hypocrisy will serve as well
To propagate a church as zeal;
As persecution and promotion
Do equally advance devotion:
So round white stones will serve, they say,
As well as eggs, to make hens lay.

Butler

404

Man differs from other animals particularly in this, that he is imitative, and acquires his rudiments of knowledge in this way; besides, the delight in imitation is universal.

Aristotle

405

The hooting fowler seldom takes much game. When a man has a project in his mind, digested and fixed by consideration, it is wise to keep it secret till the time that his designs arrive at their despatch and perfection. He is unwise who brags much either of what he will do or what he shall have, for if what he speaks of fall not out accordingly, instead of applause, a mock and scorn will follow him.

Feltham

406

What is the most profitable? Fellowship with the good. What is the worst thing in the world? The society of evil men. What is the greatest loss? Failure in one's duty. Where is the greatest peace? In truth and righteousness. Who is the hero? The man who subdues his senses. Who is the best beloved? The faithful wife. What is wealth? Knowledge. What is the most perfect happiness? Staying at home.

Bhartrihari

407

If a man says that it is right to give every one his due, and therefore thinks within his own mind that injury is due from a just man to his enemies but kindness to his friends, he was not wise who said so, for he spoke not the truth, for in no case has it appeared to be just to injure any one.[21]

Plato

408

Faith is like love, it cannot be forced. Therefore it is a dangerous operation if an attempt be made to introduce or bind it by state regulations; for, as the attempt to force love

---

[21] Cf. Matt. V, 43, 44

begets hatred, so also to compel religious belief produces rank unbelief.

Schopenhauer

409

We are like vessels tossed on the bosom of the deep; our passions are the winds that sweep us impetuously forward; each pleasure is a rock; the whole life is a wide ocean. Reason is the pilot to guide us, but often allows itself to be led astray by the storms of pride.

Metastasio

410

Empty is the house of a childless man; as empty is the mind of a bachelor; empty are all quarters of the world to an ignorant man; but poverty is total emptiness.

Hitopadesa

411

The wicked have no stability, for they do not remain in consistency with themselves; they continue friends only for a short time, rejoicing in each other's wickedness.

Aristotle

412

It is the natural disposition of all men to listen with pleasure to abuse and slander of their neighbour, and to hear with impatience those who utter praises of themselves.

Demosthenes

413

A man ought not to return evil for evil, as many think,

since at no time ought we to do an injury to our neighbour.[22]

Plato

414

In all that belongs to man you cannot find a greater wonder than memory. What a treasury of all things! What a record! What a journal of all! As if provident Nature, because she would have man circumspect, had furnished him with an account-book, to carry always with him. Yet it neither burthens nor takes up room.

Feltham

415

He who will not freely and sadly confess that he is much a fool is all a fool.

Fuller

416

The man with hoary head is not revered as aged by the gods, but only he who has true knowledge; he, though young, is old.

Manu

417

No fathers and mothers think their own children ugly, and this self-deceit is yet stronger with respect to the offspring of the mind.

Cervantes

418

In thy apparel avoid singularity, profuseness, and

---

[22] Cf. Rom. XII, 19; 1 Thess. V, 15

gaudiness. Be not too early in the fashion, nor too late. Decency is half way between affectation and neglect. The body is the shell of the soul, apparel is the husk of that shell; the husk often tells you what the kernel is.

Quarles

419

We have more faith in a well-written romance while we are reading it than in common history. The vividness of the representations in the one case more than counterbalances the mere knowledge of the truth of facts in the other.

Hazlitt

420

It is easy to lose important opportunities, and difficult to regain them; therefore when they present themselves it is the more necessary to make every effort to retain them.

Guicciardini

421

Among wonderful things is a sore-eyed man who is an oculist.

Arabic

422

Gold gives the appearance of beauty even to ugliness; but everything becomes frightful with poverty.

Boileau

423

When the scale of sensuality bears down that of reason, the baseness of our nature conducts us to most preposterous conclusions.

R. Chamberlain

424

Idleness is a great enemy to mankind. There is no friend like energy, for, if you cultivate that, it will never fail.

Bhartrihari

425

The greatest difficulties lie where we are not looking for them.

Goethe

426

We must oblige everybody as much as we can; we have often need of assistance from those inferior to ourselves.

La Fontaine

427

We magnify the wealthy man, though his parts be never so poor. The poor man we despise, be he never so well qualified. Gold is the coverlet of imperfections. It is the fool's curtain, which hides all his defects from the world.

Feltham

428

There is nothing more operative than sedulity and diligence. A man would wonder at the mighty things which have been done by degrees and gentle augmentations. Diligence and moderation are the best steps whereby to climb to any excellence, nay, it is rare that there is any other other way.

Feltham

429

In sooth, it is a shame to choose rather to be still borrowing in all places, from everybody, than to work and win.

Rabelais

430

Behaviour is a mirror in which every one shows his image.

Goethe

431

There is nothing more daring than ignorance.

Menander

432

It is not easy to stop the fire when the water is at a distance; friends at hand are better than relations afar off.

Chinese

433

The lustre of a virtuous character cannot be defaced, nor can the vices of a vicious man ever become lucid. A jewel preserves its lustre, though trodden in the mud, but a brass pot, though placed upon the head, is brass still.

Panchatantra

434

Noble birth is an accident of fortune, noble actions characterise the great.

Goldoni

435

Simplicity of character is the natural result of profound thought.

Hazlitt

436

When anyone is modest, not after praise, but after censure, then he is really so.

Richter

437

Experience has always shown, and reason shows, that affairs which depend on many seldom succeed.

Guicciardini

438

Give not thy tongue too great a liberty, lest it take thee prisoner. A word unspoken is like thy sword in thy scabbard; if vented, the sword is in another's hand.[23] If thou desire to be held wise, be so wise as to hold thy tongue.

Quarles

439

The old lose one of the greatest privileges of man, for they are no longer judged by their contemporaries.

Goethe

---

[23] Cf. 221; also Metastasio:
Voce dal fuggita
Poi richiamar non vale;
Non si trattien lo strale
Quando dall' arco uscì.
[The word that once escapes the tongue cannot be recalled; the arrow cannot be detained which has once sped from the bow.]

440

When the man of a naturally good propensity has much wealth it injures his advancement in wisdom; when a worthless man has much wealth it increases his faults.

Chinese

441

In youth a man is deluded by other ideas than those which delude him in middle life, and again in his decay he embraces other ideas.

Mahābhārata

442

To consider, Is this man of our own or an alien? is a mark of little-minded persons; but the whole earth is of kin to the generous-hearted.[24]

Panchatantra

443

Skill in advising others is easily attained by men; but to practise righteousness themselves is what only a few can succeed in doing.

Hitopadesa

444

Hast thou not perfect excellence, 'tis best
To keep thy tongue in silence, for 'tis this
Which shames a man; as lightness does attest
The nut is empty, nor of value is.

Sa'dī

---

[24] Cf. Luke, X, 29, ff.

445

Understand a man by his deeds and words; the impressions of others lead to false judgment.

Talmud

446

A man of feeble character resembles a reed that bends with every gust of wind.

Māgha

447

There is no fire like passion; there is no shark like hatred; there is no snare like folly; there is no torrent like greed.

Dhammapada

448

Commit a sin twice, and it will not seem to thee a sin.

Talmud

449

Liberality attended with mild language; learning without pride; valour united with mercy; wealth accompanied with a generous contempt of it—these four qualities are with difficulty acquired.

Hitopadesa

450

Inquire about your neighbour before you build, and about your companions before you travel.

Arabic

451

Though you may yourself abound in treasure, teach your son some handicraft; for a heavy purse of gold and silver may run to waste, but the purse of the artisan's industry can never get empty.

Sa'dī

452

It is an observation no less just than common that there is no stronger test of a man's real character than power and authority, exciting, as they do, every passion, and discovering every latent vice.

Plutarch

453

Rather skin a carcass for pay in the public streets than be idly dependent on charity.

Talmud

454

Knowledge produces mildness of speech; mildness of speech, a good character; a good character, wealth; wealth, if virtuous actions attend it, happiness.

Hitopadesa

455

O how wonderful is the human voice! It is indeed the organ of the soul. The intellect of man sits enshrined visibly upon his forehead and in his eye; and the heart of man is written upon his countenance. But the soul reveals itself in the voice only, as God revealed himself to the prophet in the still small voice, and in a voice from the Burning Bush. The soul of man is audible, not visible. A sound alone betrays the flowing of the eternal fountain invisible to man.

Longfellow

456

Every gift, though small, is in reality great, if it be given with affection.[25]

Philemon

457

Good words, good deeds, and beautiful expressions
A wise man ever culls from every quarter,
E'en as a gleaner gathers ears of corn.

Mahābhārata

458

In poverty and other misfortunes of life men think friends to be their only refuge. The young they keep out of mischief, to the old they are a comfort and aid in their weakness, and those in the prime of life they incite to noble deeds.

Aristotle

459

Heed not the flatterer's fulsome talk,
He from thee hopes some trifle to obtain;
Thou wilt, shouldst thou his wishes baulk,
Ten hundred times as much of censure gain.

Sa'dī

460

By the fall of water-drops the pot is filled: such is the increase of riches, of knowledge, and of virtue.

Hitopadesa

---

[25] See also 80

461

We deliberate about the parcels of life, but not about life itself, and so we arrive all unawares at its different epochs, and have the trouble of beginning all again. And so finally it is that we do not walk as men confidently towards death, but let death come suddenly upon us.

Seneca

462

It is no very good symptom, either of nations or individuals, that they deal much in vaticination. Happy men are full of the present, for its bounty suffices them; and wise men also, for its duties engage them. Our grand business undoubtedly is not to see what lies dimly at a distance, but to do what clearly lies at hand.

Carlyle

463

Law does not put the least restraint
Upon our freedom, but maintain'st;
Or, if it does, 'tis for our good,
To give us freer latitude:
For wholesome laws preserve us free,
By stinting of our liberty.

Butler

464

It is only necessary to grow old in order to become more indulgent. I see no fault committed that I have not been myself inclined to.

Goethe

465

Even a blockhead may respect inspire,
So long as he is suitably attired;

A fool may gain esteem among the wise,
So long as he has sense to hold his tongue.

Hitopadesa

466

A wise man should never resolve upon anything, at least, never let the world know his resolution, for if he cannot reach that he is ashamed.[26]

Selden

467

Men's minds are generally ingenious in palliating guilt in themselves.

Livy

468

Prosperity is acquired by exertion, and there is no fruit for him who doth not exert himself: the fawns go not into the mouth of a sleeping lion.

Hitopadesa

469

Wickedness, by whomsoever committed, is odious, but most of all in men of learning; for learning is the weapon with which Satan is combated, and when a man is made captive with arms in his hand his shame is more excessive.

Sa'dī

470

He that will give himself to all manner of ways to get money may be rich; so he that lets fly all he knows or thinks may by chance be satirically witty. Honesty

---

[26] See 406

sometimes keeps a man from growing rich, and civility from being witty.

Selden

471

Men are not rich or poor according to what they possess but to what they desire. The only rich man is he that with content enjoys a competence.

R. Chamberlain

472

Poverty is not dishonourable in itself, but only when it arises from idleness, intemperance, extravagance, and folly.

Plutarch

473

Do nothing rashly; want of circumspection is the chief cause of failure and disaster. Fortune, wise lover of the wise, selects him for her lord who ere he acts reflects.

Bhāravi

474

First think, and if thy thoughts approve thy will,
Then speak, and after, what thou speak'st fulfil.

Randolph

475

It cannot but be injurious to the human mind never to be called into effort: the habit of receiving pleasure without any exertion of thought, by the mere excitement of curiosity, and sensibility, may be justly ranked among the worst effects of habitual novel-reading.

Coleridge

476

Patience is the chiefest fruit of study; a man that strives to make himself different from other men by much reading gains this chiefest good, that in all fortunes he hath something to entertain and comfort himself withal.

Selden

477

Friendship throws a greater lustre on prosperity, while it lightens adversity by sharing in its griefs and troubles.

Cicero

478

There is nothing more becoming a wise man than to make choice of friends, for by them thou shalt be judged what thou art. Let them therefore be wise and virtuous, and none of those that follow thee for gain; but make election rather of thy betters than thy inferiors; shunning always such as are poor and needy, for if thou givest twenty gifts and refuse to do the like but once, all that thou hast done will be lost, and such men will become thy mortal enemies.

Sir W. Raleigh, to his Son

479

Learning is like Scanderbeg's sword, either good or bad according to him who hath it: an excellent weapon, if well used; otherwise, like a sharp razor in the hand of a child.

R. Chamberlain

480

The greater part of mankind employ their first years to make their last miserable.

La Bruyère

481

I hate the miser, whose unsocial breast
Locks from the world his useless stores.
Wealth by the bounteous only is enjoyed,
Whose treasures, in diffusive good employed,
The rich return of fame and friends procure,
And 'gainst a sad reverse a safe retreat secure.

Pindar

482

Wisdom alone is the true and unalloyed coin for which we ought to exchange all things, for this and with this everything is bought and sold—fortitude, temperance, and justice; in a word, true virtue subsists with wisdom.

Plato

483

If thou intendest to do a good act, do it quickly, and then thou wilt excite gratitude; a favour if it be slow in being conferred causes ingratitude.

Ausonius

484

'Tis those who reverence the old
That are the men versed in the Faith;
Worthy of praise while in this life,
And happy in the life to come.

Buddhist

485

Low-minded men are occupied solely with their own affairs, but noble-minded men take special interest in the affairs of others. The submarine fire drinks up the ocean, to fill its insatiable interior; the rain-cloud, that it may relieve the drought of the earth, burnt up by the hot season.

Bhartrihari

486

Those men are wise who do not desire the unattainable, who do not love to mourn over what is lost, and are not overwhelmed by calamities.

Mahābhārata

487

Let him take heart who does advance, even in the smallest degree.

Plato

488

A truly great man never puts away the simplicity of a child.[27]

Chinese

489

If thou desirest ease in this life, keep thy secrets undisclosed, like the modest rosebud. Take warning from that lovely flower, which, by expanding its hitherto hidden beauties when in full bloom, gives its leaves and its happiness to the winds.

Persian

490

A husband is the chief ornament of a wife, though she have

---

[27] Cf. Pope, in his Epitaph on the poet Gay:
Of manners gentle, of affections mild;
In wit a man, simplicity, a child.

no other ornament; but, though adorned, without a husband she has no ornaments.

Hitopadesa

491

He who has more learning than goodness is like a tree with many branches and few roots, which the first wind throws down; whilst he whose works are greater than his knowledge is like a tree with many roots and fewer branches, which all the winds of heaven cannot uproot.

Talmud

492

He that would build lastingly must lay his foundation low. The proud man, like the early shoots of a new-felled coppice, thrusts out full of sap, green in leaves, and fresh in colour, but bruises and breaks with every wind, is nipped with every little cold, and, being top-heavy, is wholly unfit for use. Whereas the humble man retains it in the root, can abide the winter's killing blast, the ruffling concussions of the wind, and can endure far more than that which appears so flourishing.

Feltham

493

The man who has not anything to boast of but his illustrious ancestors is like a potato—the only good belonging to him is underground.

Sir Thos. Overbury

494

When men will not be reasoned out of a vanity, they must be ridiculed out of it.

L'Estrange

495

Women are ever in extremes, they are either better or worse than men.

La Bruyère

496

An absent friend gives us friendly company when we are well assured of his happiness.

Goethe

497

The man of worth is really great without being proud; the mean man is proud without being really great.

Chinese

498

Liberality consists less in giving much than in giving at the right moment.

La Bruyère

499

Outward perfection without inward goodness sets but the blacker dye on the mind's deformity.

R. Chamberlain

500

As a solid rock is not shaken by the wind, so wise men falter not amidst blame or praise.

Dhammapada

501

Of what avail is the praise or censure of the vulgar, who make a useless noise like a senseless crow in a forest?

Mahābhārata

502

Hark! here the sound of lute so sweet,
And there the voice of wailing loud;
Here scholars grave in conclave meet,
There howls the brawling drunken crowd;
Here, charming maidens full of glee,
There, tottering, withered dames we see.
Such light! Such shade! I cannot tell,
If here we live in heaven or hell.

Bhartrihari

503

The every-day cares and duties which men call drudgery are the weights and counterpoises of the clock of Time, giving its pendulum a true vibration, and its hands a regular motion; and when they cease to hang upon the wheels, the pendulum no longer sways, the hands no longer move, the clock stands still.

Longfellow

504

A man of little learning deems that little a great deal; a frog, never having seen the ocean, considers its well a great sea.

Burmese

505

Trust not thy secret to a confidant, for he too will have his associates and friends; and it will spread abroad through the whole city, and men will call thee weak-headed.

Firdausī

506

Labour like a man, and be ready in doing kindnesses. He is a good-for-nothing fellow who eateth by the toil of another's hand.

Sa'dī[28]

507

Let every man sweep the snow from before his own doors, and not busy himself about the frost on his neighbour's tiles.

Chinese

508

With knowledge, say, what other wealth
Can vie, which neither thieves by stealth
Can take, nor kinsmen make their prey,
Which, lavished, never wastes away.

Sanskrit

509

Women's wealth is beauty, learning, that of men.

Burmese

510

Prosperity attends the lion-hearted man who exerts himself, while we say, destiny will ensure it. Laying aside destiny, show manly fortitude by thy own strength: if thou

---

[28] See also 429, 453

endeavour, and thy endeavours fail of success, what crime is there in failing?

Hitopadesa

511

Spare not, nor spend too much, be this thy care,
Spare but to spend, and only spend to spare.
Who spends too much may want, and so complain;
But he spends best that spares to spend again.

Randolph

512

Everything that is acknowledges the blessing of existence. Shalt not thou, by a similar acknowledgment, be happy? If thou pay due attention to sounds, thou shalt hear the praise of the Creator celebrated by the whole creation.

Nakhshabī

513

The attribute most noble of the hand
Is readiness in giving; of the head,
Bending before a teacher; of the mouth,
Veracious speaking; of a victor's arms,
Undaunted valour; of the inner heart,
Pureness the most unsullied; of the ears,
Delight in hearing and receiving truth—These
are adornments of high-minded men,
Better than all the majesty of Empire.

Bhartrihari

514

The mere reality of life would be inconceivably poor without the charm of fancy, which brings in its bosom as many vain fears as idle hopes, but lends much oftener to the illusions it calls up a gay flattering hue than one which inspires terror.

Von Humboldt

515

Stupidity has its sublime as well as genius, and he who carries that quality to absurdity has reached it, which is always a source of pleasure to sensible people.

Wieland

516

It is curious to note the old sea-margins of human thought. Each subsiding century reveals some new mystery; we build where monsters used to hide themselves.

Longfellow

517

Women never reason and therefore they are, comparatively, seldom wrong. They judge instinctively of what falls under their immediate observation or experience, and do not trouble themselves about remote or doubtful consequences. If they make no profound discoveries, they do not involve themselves in gross absurdities. It is only by the help of reason and logical inference, according to Hobbes, that "man becomes excellently wise or excellently foolish."

Hazlitt

518

Reprove not in their wrath incensèd men,
Good counsel comes clean out of season then;
But when his fury is appeased and past,
He will conceive his fault and mend at last:
When he is cool and calm, then utter it;
No man gives physic in the midst o' th' fit.

Randolph

519

It is not flesh and blood, it is the heart, that makes fathers and sons.

Schiller

520

Discontent is like ink poured into water, which fills the whole fountain full of blackness. It casts a cloud over the mind, and renders it more occupied about the evil which disquiets it than about the means of removing it.

Feltham

521

We are accustomed to see men deride what they do not understand, and snarl at the good and beautiful because it lies beyond their sympathies.

Goethe

522

A just and reasonable modesty does not only recommend eloquence, but sets off every talent which a man can be possessed of. It heightens all the virtues which it accompanies; like the shades of paintings, it raises and rounds every figure, and makes the colours more beautiful, though not so glowing as they would be without it.

Addison

523

Happy the man who lives at home, making it his business to regulate his desires.

La Fontaine

524

It is true that men are no fit judges of themselves, because commonly they are partial to their own cause; yet it is as true that he who will dispose himself to judge indifferently of himself can do it better than any body else, because a man can see farther into his own mind and heart than any one else can.

Harrington

525

Envy is a vice that would pose a man to tell what it should be liked for. Other vices we assume for that we falsely suppose they bring us either pleasure, profit, or honour. But in envy who is it can find any of these? Instead of pleasure, we vex and gall ourselves. Like cankered brass, it only eats itself, nay, discolours and renders it noisome. When some one told Agis that those of his neighbour's family did envy him, "Why, then," says he, "they have a double vexation—one, with their own evil, the other, at my prosperity."

Feltham

526

The most silent people are generally those who think most highly of themselves. They fancy themselves superior to every one else, and, not being sure of making good their secret pretensions, decline entering the lists altogether. Thus they "lay the flattering unction to their souls" that they could have said better things than others, or that the conversation was beneath them.

Hazlitt

527

It is commonly a dangerous thing for a man to have more sense than his neighbours. Socrates paid for his superiority with his life; and if Aristotle saved his skin, accused as he was of heresy by the chief priest Eurymedon, it was because he took to his heels in time.

Wieland

528

Flattery may be considered as a mode of companionship, degrading but profitable to him who flatters.

Theophrastus

529

Rich presents, though profusely given, Are not so dear to righteous Heaven As gifts by honest gains supplied, Though small, which faith hath sanctified.

Mahābhārata

530

To-day is thine to spend, but not to-morrow;
Counting on morrows breedeth bankrupt sorrow:
O squander not this breath that Heaven hath lent thee;
Make not too sure another breath to borrow.

Omar Khayyām

531

Leave not the business of to-day to be done to-morrow; for who knoweth what may be thy condition to-morrow? The rose-garden, which to-day is full of flowers, when to-morrow thou wouldst pluck a rose, may not afford thee one.

Firdausī

532

Virtue beameth from a generous spirit as light from the moon, or as brilliancy from Jupiter.

Nizāmī

533

The worth of a horse is known by its speed, the value of

oxen by their carrying power, the worth of a cow by its milk-giving capacity, and that of a wise man by his speech.

Burmese

534

Men of genius are often dull and inert in society, as the blazing meteor when it descends to earth is only a stone.

Longfellow

535

If a man die young he hath left us at dinner; it is bed-time with a man of three score and ten; and he that lives a hundred years hath walked a mile after supper. This life is but one day of three meals, or one meal of three courses— childhood, youth, and old age. To sup well is to live well, and that's the way to sleep well.

Overbury

536

There is nothing keeps longer than a middling fortune, and nothing melts away sooner than a great one. Poverty treads upon the heels of great and unexpected riches.

La Bruyère

537

Society is a more level surface than we imagine. Wise men or absolute fools are hard to be met with, as there are few giants or dwarfs. The heaviest charge we can bring against the general texture of society is that it is commonplace. Our fancied superiority to others is in some one thing which we think most of because we excel in it, or have paid most attention to it; whilst we overlook their superiority to us in something else which they set equal and exclusive store by.

Hazlitt

538

It is resignation and contentment that are best calculated to lead us safely through life. Whoever has not sufficient power to endure privations, and even suffering, can never feel that he is armour-proof against painful emotions; nay, he must attribute to himself, or at least to the morbid sensitiveness of his nature, every disagreeable feeling he may suffer.

Von Humboldt

539

Petrarch observes, that we change language, habits, laws, customs, manners, but not vices, not diseases, not the symptoms of folly and madness—they are still the same. And as a river, we see, keeps the like name and place, but not water, and yet ever runs, our times and persons alter, vices are the same, and ever be. Look how nightingales sang of old, cocks crowed, kine lowed, sheep bleated, sparrows chirped, dogs barked, so they do still: we keep our madness still, play the fool still; we are of the same humours and inclinations as our predecessors were; you shall find us all alike, much as one, we and our sons, and so shall our posterity continue to the last.

Burton

540

The mother of the useful arts is necessity, that of the fine arts is luxury; for father the former have intellect, the latter, genius, which itself is a kind of luxury.

Schopenhauer

541

The fool who knows his foolishness is wise so far, at least; but a fool who thinks himself wise, he is called a fool indeed.

Dhammapada

542

He who mixes with unclean things becomes unclean himself; he whose associations are pure becomes purer each day.

Talmud

543

Heaven's gate is narrow and minute,[29]
It cannot be perceived by foolish men,
Blinded by vain illusions of the world.
E'en the clear-sighted, who discern the way
And seek to enter, find the portal barred
And hard to be unlocked. Its massive bolts
Are pride and passion, avarice and lust.

Mahābhārata

544

Eschew that friend, if thou art wise, who consorts with thy enemies.

Sa'dī

545

Who can tell
Men's hearts? The purest comprehend
Such contradictions, and can blend
The force to bear, the power to feel,
The tender bud, the tempered steel.

Hindu Drama

546

Whosoever hath not knowledge, and benevolence, and

---

[29] Cf. Matt. VII, 14

piety knoweth nothing of reality, and dwelleth only in semblance.

Sa'dī

547

If thou shouldst find thy friend in the wrong reprove him secretly, but in the presence of company praise him.

Arabic

548

Modesty is attended with profit, arrogance brings on destruction.

Chinese

549

The greatest hatred, like the greatest virtue and the worst dogs, is quiet.

Richter

550

Is a preface exquisitely written? No literary morsel is more delicious. Is the author inveterately dull? It is a kind of preparatory information, which may be very useful. It argues a deficiency of taste to turn over an elaborate preface unread: for it is the attar of the author's roses, every drop distilled at an immense cost. It is the reason of the reasoning, and the folly of the foolish.

Isaac D'Israeli

551

Vulgar prejudices are those which arise out of accident, ignorance, or authority; natural prejudices are those which arise out of the constitution of the human mind itself.

Hazlitt

552

Lament not Fortune's mutability,
And seize her fickle favours ere they flee;
If others never mourned departed bliss,
How should a turn of Fortune come to thee?

Omar Khayyām

553

Harsh reproof is like a violent storm, soon washed down
the channel; but friendly admonitions, like a small shower,
pierce deep, and bring forth better reformation.

R. Chamberlain

554

There are braying men in the world as well as braying
asses; for what's loud and senseless talking, huffing, and
swearing any other than a more fashionable way of
braying?

L'Estrange

555

All wit and fancy, like a diamond,
The more exact and curious 'tis ground,
Is forced for every carat to abate
As much of value as it wants in weight.

Butler

556

Listen, if you would learn; be silent, if you would be safe.

Arabic

557

All such distinctions as tend to set the orders of the state at a distance from each other are equally subversive of liberty and concord.

Livy

558

No man is the wiser for his learning. It may administer matter to work in, or objects to work upon, but wit and wisdom are born with a man.

Selden

559

Those who are guided by reason are generally successful in their plans; those who are rash and precipitate seldom enjoy the favour of the gods.

Herodotus

560

Whosoever lends a greedy ear to a slanderous report is either himself of a radically bad disposition or a mere child in sense.

Menander

561

A foolish man in wealth and authority is like a weak-timbered house with a too-ponderous roof.

R. Chamberlain

562

A lively blockhead in company is a public benefit. Silence or dulness by the side of folly looks like wisdom.

Hazlitt

563

Eminent positions make eminent men greater and little men less.

La Bruyère

564

Scratch yourself with your own nails; always do your own business, and when you intend asking for a service, go to a person who can appreciate your merit.

Arabic

565

The beauty of some women has days and seasons, depending upon accidents which diminish or increase it; nay, the very passions of the mind naturally improve or impair it, and very often utterly destroy it.

Cervantes

566

No joy in nature is so sublimely affecting as the joy of a mother at the good fortune of a child.

Richter

567

Want and sorrow are the gifts which folly earns for itself.

Schubert

568

In character, in manners, in style, in all things, the supreme excellence is simplicity.

Longfellow

569

Those who cause dissensions in order to injure other people are preparing pitfalls for their own ruin.

Chinese

570

Such deeds as thou with fear and grief
Wouldst, on a sick-bed laid, recall,
In youth and health eschew them all,
Remembering life is frail and brief.

Mahābhārata

571

A man should not keep company with one whose character, family, and abode are unknown.

Panchatantra

572

Sit not down to the table before thy stomach is empty, and rise before thou hast filled it.

Arabic

573

If thou be rich, strive to command thy money, lest it command thee.

Quarles

574

In all companies there are more fools than wise men, and the greater part always gets the better of the wiser.

Rabelais

575

Talents are best nurtured in solitude; character is best formed in the stormy billows of the world.

Goethe

576

No one ought to despond in adverse circumstances, for they may turn out to be the cause of good to us.[30]

Menander

577

The constant man loses not his virtue in misfortune. A torch may point towards the ground, but its flame will still point upwards.

Bhartrihari

578

A man should never despise himself, for brilliant success never attends on the man who is contemned by himself.

Mahābhārata

579

It is the character of a simpleton to be a bore. A man of sense sees at once whether he is welcome or tiresome; he knows to withdraw the moment that precedes that in which he would be in the least in the way.

La Bruyère

580

The man of first rate excellence is virtuous in spite of

---

[30] Cf. Job V, 17; Heb. XII, 6

instruction; he of the middle class is so after instruction; the lowest order of men are vicious in spite of instruction.

Chinese

581

Not to attend at the door of the wealthy, and not to use the voice of petition—these constitute the best life of a man.

Hitopadesa

582

What a man can do and suffer is unknown to himself till some occasion presents itself which draws out the hidden power. Just as one sees not in the water of an unruffled pond the fury and roar with which it can dash down a steep rock without injury to itself, or how high it is capable of rising; or as little as one can suspect the latent heat in ice-cold water.

Schopenhauer

583

Comprehensive talkers are apt to be tiresome when we are not athirst for information; but, to be quite fair, we must admit that superior reticence is a good deal due to lack of matter. Speech is often barren, but silence also does not necessarily brood over a full nest. Your still fowl, blinking at you without remark, may all the while be sitting on one addled nest-egg; and, when it takes to cackling, will have nothing to announce but that addled delusion.

George Eliot

584

The sage who engages in controversy with ignorant people must not expect to be treated with honour; and if a fool should overpower a philosopher by his loquacity it is not to be wondered at, for a common stone will break a jewel.

Sa'dī

585

Success is like a lovely woman, wooed by many men, but folded in the arms of him alone who, free from over-zeal, firmly persists and calmly perseveres.

Bhāravi

586

A feverish display of over-zeal,
At the first outset, is an obstacle
To all success; water, however cold,
Will penetrate the ground by slow degrees.

Hitopadesa

587

Treat no one with disdain; with patience bear
Reviling language; with an angry man
Be never angry; blessings give for curses.[31]

Manu

588

E'en as a traveller, meeting with the shade
Of some o'erhanging tree, awhile reposes,
Then leaves its shelter to pursue his way,
So men meet friends, then part with them for
ever.

Hitopadesa

589

Single is every living creature born,
Single he passes to another world,
Single he eats the fruit of evil deeds,
Single, the fruit of good; and when he leaves
His body, like a log or heap of clay,

---

[31] Cf. Matt. V, II, 44

Upon the ground, his kinsmen walk away:
Virtue alone stays by him at the tomb,
And bears him through the dreary, trackless
gloom.

Manu